TIME TRAVEL SLEEPOVER

KNIGHTS & CASTLES

EAT, SLEEP, AND PARTY IN THE MIDDLE AGES!

◆

WRITTEN BY

TIMOTHY KNAPMAN

ILLUSTRATED BY

MATT ROBERTSON

To Christopher and Charlotte with love — T. K.   **To Will and Kitty — M. R.**

© 2024 Quarto Publishing Group USA Inc.
Illustration © 2024 Matt Robertson

Matt Robertson has asserted his right to be identified as the illustrator of this work.

Senior Designer: Sarah Chapman-Suire
Commissioning Editor: Carly Madden
Editor: Clare Whitston
History Consultant: Kathryn Hurlock
Inclusivity Consultant: Lisa Davis
Creative Director: Malena Stojić
Associate Publisher: Rhiannon Findlay

First published in 2024 by Happy Yak,
an imprint of The Quarto Group.
100 Cummings Center, Suite 265D, Beverly, MA 01915, USA.
T (978) 282-9590 F (978) 283-2742
www.quarto.com

ISBN 978 0 7112 8727 3

Manufactured in Guangdong, China TT042024

9 8 7 6 5 4 3 2 1

FSC MIX Paper | Supporting responsible forestry
www.fsc.org FSC® C016973

CONTENTS

Ouch!

Say hello to our TIME TRAVELERS!

JAKE

Interests: stomping around in armor, making a lot of noise

If you could go anywhere in history: I'd go to the Middle Ages, and be a knight

What you hope to get from this adventure: I'd like to give jousting a try!

LULA

Interests: having an adventure, of course!

If you could go anywhere in history: I'd go to a time where kids got to charge around on horseback

What you hope to get from this adventure: to find out what knights were REALLY like!

CLAWDIA

Interests: lying on sunny windowsills

If you could go anywhere in history: I'd go somewhere with a lot of mice

What you hope to get from this adventure: a bellyful of mice

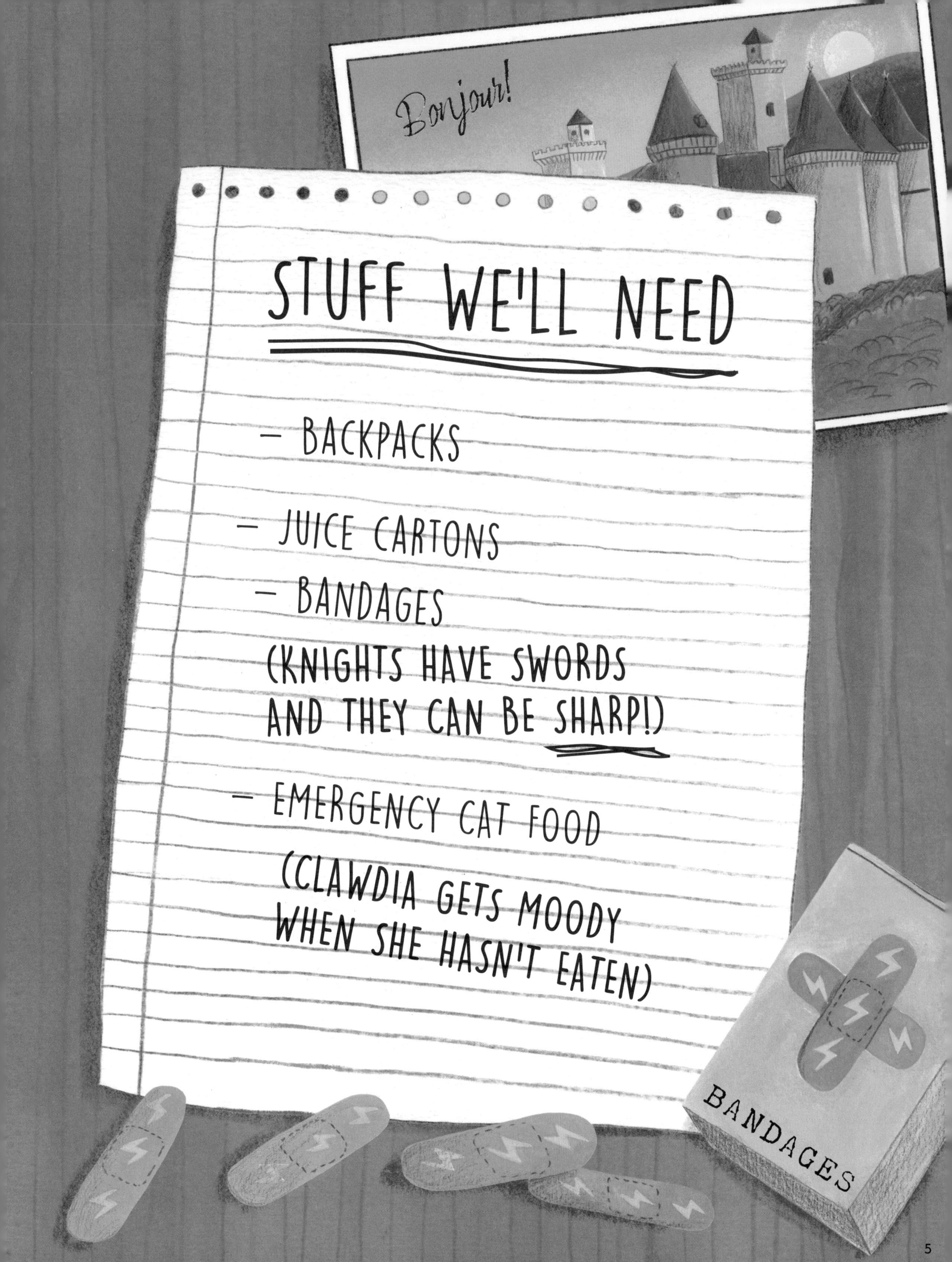

STUFF WE'LL NEED

- BACKPACKS

- JUICE CARTONS

- BANDAGES
(KNIGHTS HAVE SWORDS
AND THEY CAN BE SHARP!)

- EMERGENCY CAT FOOD
(CLAWDIA GETS MOODY
WHEN SHE HASN'T EATEN)

Bonjour!

BANDAGES

HERE WE GO!
KNIGHTS AND CASTLES

Our friends have traveled back to the Middle Ages—the time of knights and castles!

"They don't seem to like cats much around here," says Jake.

"Maybe they're allergic," says Lula.

"Cats are thought to bring bad luck," explains one child.

"But they're also useful for catching mice," says another. "Anyway, *we* like cats."

"Welcome to the Middle Ages!"

"Our cat's called Clawdia," says Lula. "I'm Lula and this is Jake."

"I'm Eloise and this is my brother Hubert," says the girl.

"The baron, who owns this castle, has just returned home," says Hubert. "There's going to be a feast tonight to celebrate. Everyone is very busy!"

...YOU'RE THERE!

Aaaarrrgh! A CAT!

Huh?

Are you ready?
Time travel's easy—you just have to do
THE TIME TRAVEL SHIMMY.
You do a little wiggle and...
...you touch the ground.
Then wrinkle your nose while you spin around.

Whoosh!

You shake your hips.

Then you jump off the ground.
And just like that...

MAKE YOURSELF AT HOME
INSIDE THE CASTLE

Eloise and Hubert invite Lula and Jake inside the castle keep. The keep is the center of the castle and the safest place to be.

"It's very cold and dark," says Jake. "Where's the light switch?"

"They don't have electricity," says Lula. "Or central heating—brrr!"

"We use candles for light, fire for heat, and wall hangings to keep the drafts out," says Hubert.

"No wonder it's so hard to keep warm!" says Jake.

 GOOD NEWS!

Castles had toilets, called garderobes.

 BAD NEWS!

They were just holes in the floor, covered with planks of wood.

 GOOD NEWS!

They were high up so anything smelly fell a long way down.

 BAD NEWS!

Watch out if you're underneath it when it lands!

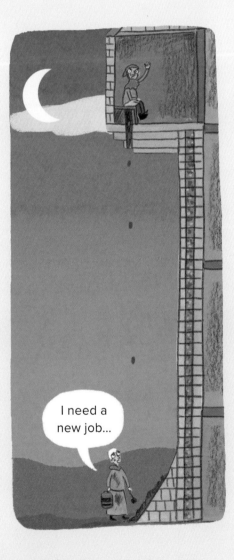

I need a new job...

When there was enough waste, the poop was taken away at night by someone called a gong farmer, who then sold it to farmers to fertilize their fields.

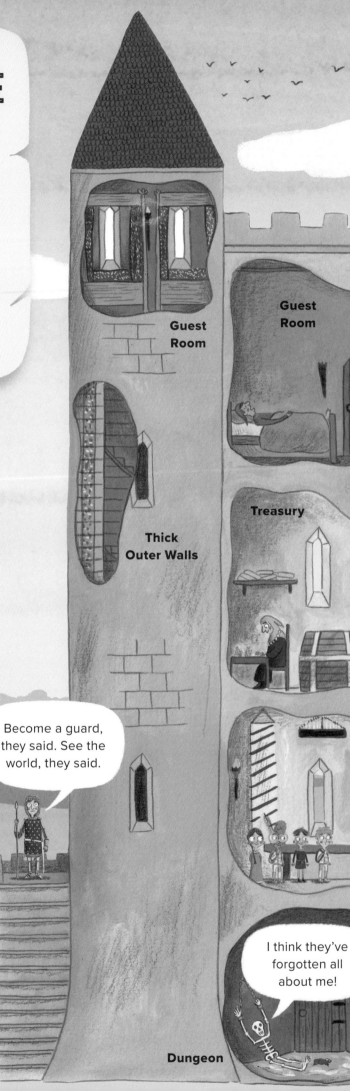

Guest Room

Guest Room

Treasury

Thick Outer Walls

Become a guard, they said. See the world, they said.

I think they've forgotten all about me!

Dungeon

MAKEOVER TIME!
CLOTHES AND HAIRSTYLES

While the baron is in the bath, the kids sneak into his chambers to look at his clothes.

"You'll need clothes from our time if you want to blend in," says Eloise.

All these layers would be a lot warmer than pajamas!

You can't just wear what you like. There are special laws that say only important people can dress in fine clothes.

This is top-quality cloth! If I nibble it a bit, it'll make perfect bedding for me!

"What does everyone else wear?" asks Jake.

"They have a simpler outfit they wear every day," says Hubert.

"It's a hoodie—cool! But what's it made of?" asks Jake.

"Rough wool and linen, so it's very itchy," says Hubert.

I'll be scratching all day long!

16

"Our dresses have to cover our arms and legs. Only people doing the laundry show their bare arms!" says Eloise.

"What about my lovely hair?" asks Lula.

"Married women cover their hair," says Eloise.

Some wear what's called a wimple.

I can't see!

You're wearing it the wrong way round!

Don't forget your braies, Jake.

I draw the line at wearing medieval underpants!

GOOD NEWS!

You're a well-dressed young man in the Middle Ages!

BAD NEWS!

Your super-cool pointy shoes—called crakows—are impossible to walk in.

GOOD NEWS!

Your super-short tunic is very fashionable.

BAD NEWS!

Your tunic is so short, your butt gets cold!

KNIGHTS' TOGS
DRESSED TO KILL

Jake and Lula can't wait any longer to find out about suits of armor, so Hubert and Eloise take them to try some on.

1. First you wear a gambeson—a quilted shirt filled with feathers.

Achoo! I'm allergic to feathers.

2. Over that, a shirt of chain mail. You roll it on, like a woolly sweater.

It's a very heavy sweater!

3. Then the coat of steel plates.

I think I'm going to fall over.

4. Then the helmet.

I can't see and everything hurts!

5. Finally, the surcoat to keep the sun off your armor.

Helllpppp!!

The emblem on the surcoat shows whose side you're on in a battle.

Who knew a little surcoat could be so heavy?

Help!

How does a knight go to the toilet?

Very carefully.

Armor is cleaned with a mixture of sand and pee to stop it from rusting.

Eeewww! Get this off me!

The only armor I need is a metal cup!

Each piece of armor has a special name.

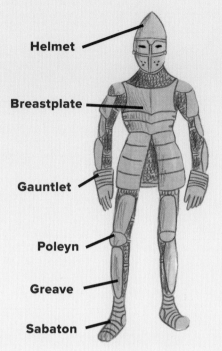

Helmet

Breastplate

Gauntlet

Poleyn

Greave

Sabaton

Knights wear special armor for jousting (fighting on horseback for sport and honor).

The shoulder plate protects a knight from their opponent's lance.

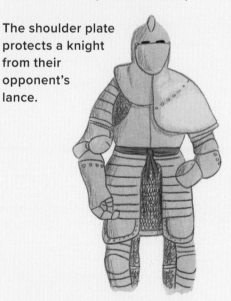

"Some armor allowed a knight to be screwed into their saddle so they wouldn't fall off," Hubert says.

"But that's cheating!" Lula says.

"That's what the king thought, so he banned it."

21

UNDER ATTACK!
DEFENDING THE CASTLE

Jake and Lula ask what would happen if the castle was attacked. François is still busy ordering people about, but he is an expert on defending the castle so he stops to explain.

"The attackers use catapults to throw heavy objects to break down the castle. This trebuchet can chuck large blocks nearly 1,000 feet!" says François.

"So what do you do?" asks Lula.

"Duck!" shouts François.

Our archers are protected by these tiny arrow slits as they shoot at the attackers.

Ouch!

Well, they started it!

Cats, I don't mind, but I am allergic to sieges.

We're not FELINE so good either!

"Sometimes attackers try to smash the front door down with a battering ram, but defenders can throw boiling oil from the gatehouse," says François.

"I think I'd decide to come again another day," says Jake.

"How do knights defend the castle?" Jake asks.

"They fight on horseback, and that's not much use in a siege," says Hubert.

"But castles have a secret back door," says François, "so that soldiers, including knights, can sneak out and ambush the attackers from behind."

"Ripples on the water in this bowl tell us that someone's tunneling under the castle to plant a bomb," explains François.

"I just thought the defenders might need to wash up," says Jake.

"A belfry, or siege tower, can hold hundreds of soldiers, protecting them until they swarm over the battlements," says François.

"Archers firing flaming arrows might be able to deter the enemy before they reach the castle walls," says Eloise.

The baron and his family eat pandemain—white bread, made from wheat flour that has been sifted two or three times. Most people eat darker bread made with rye flour.

You could have some yummy lampreys. They're like eels—so juicy!

Only if we can cover them in ketchup.

What's ketchup?

You don't have ketchup?! I want to go home!!

Large animals are roasted over open fires. They have to be turned constantly—it's hard work!

Most people eat pottage (thick vegetable soup), bread, milk, cheese, and a little bacon.

 GOOD NEWS!

It's dinnertime in the Middle Ages!

 BAD NEWS!

There are no forks and no plates—people use knives and spoons and eat off pieces of stale bread called trenchers.

 **GOOD NEWS!**

There are fewer dishes to wash!

KNIGHT SCHOOL
PART ONE: PAGE TO SQUIRE

It's too hot in the kitchen for Lula and Jake. They go outside to cool off and see two knights practicing sword fighting.

"I want to become a knight," says Jake.

"And me!" says Lula. "I bet I'd make a better knight than you!"

"Becoming a knight takes time," says Hubert, "and you start young..."

Age 7–13 You are sent to a rich household to be a page. Pages have to run errands and learn to obey orders...

Bring me a drink from the kitchens, page.

What, now?!

Oh, and one more thing...

!!!!

...and NOT complain!

Is this really how we get to become knights?

Hey, less talking, you!

KNIGHT SCHOOL
PART TWO: LEARNING SKILLS

Jake and Lula are fed up with having to look after their knights all the time.

"When do WE get to do the fun stuff?" asks Jake.

"Being a squire isn't just about taking care of your knight," says Hubert. "You are also training to become a knight yourself one day."

"But it's hard work," says Eloise. "You need to be fit and strong."

Squires are taught how to loose an arrow from a bow.

Squires learn to fight with blunt or even wooden swords. They also have a small shield called a buckler, for protection.

Squires learn how to ride a horse with one hand free, so they can still fight. They practice aiming their lance at a target called a quintain.

Squires must hit the shield and then ride away before the bag swings around and hits them on the head!

The Ceremony

At last, when squires are about **21** years old and have mastered all the skills required, they are made knights in a special ceremony.

The night before, the squire has a nice, cold bath.

Hooray! No more cleaning armor with pee!

No way! It's freezing!

Then the squire puts on a white tunic and stays up all night praying in the castle chapel.

But it's the middle of the afternoon!

Can we just skip to the next bit?

The next morning, the squire kneels before their lord, who "dubs" them by touching their shoulder or neck with the blunt side of a sword.

I'd like to keep my ears!

Be careful, Hubert!

TIME FOR SCHOOL!
LESSONS

Becoming a knight turns out to be much harder than Jake and Lula expected.

"Maybe going to school would be easier than training to be a knight," says Jake. "As long as we don't have to do difficult math."

"You'd prefer lessons to quintain practice?" says Hubert.

"You don't get bashed on the head with a heavy sandbag at school," says Lula.

"Maybe not," says Eloise, "but the castle chaplain who teaches us is very strict."

The children of craftspeople, such as carpenters or stonemasons, learn their trades by helping their families.

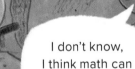

Ouch! I'd rather do difficult math than this!

I don't know, I think math can be painful too!

Like the children of merchants, the children of craftspeople also learn enough reading, writing, and arithmetic so they can keep business records.

GOOD NEWS!

You're a successful stonemason. People want you to decorate important buildings.

4+1-2=??

BAD NEWS!

You need to figure out how much money to charge for the work, but you don't have a calculator.

GOOD NEWS!

You can use a wooden counting frame called an abacus instead.

BAD NEWS!

It can only do simple calculations—it can't help with difficult math!

I don't know what this adds up to.

Schooling outside the home is often run by the Church. A lot of teaching is done by priests, and occasionally monks and nuns.

"What's this language?" says Jake.

"It's Latin, which is the language we're taught in and the language of the Catholic Church. It's understood in many countries," says Eloise.

"In class, we might still talk in our own language, but the teachers don't like it," says Hubert.

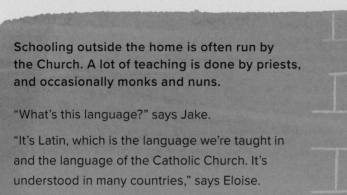

What's the Latin for "dinnertime"?

The children of privileged people such as kings, queens, and barons are taught at home by personal tutors. Less attention is paid to the education of girls, though they are still taught how to run a household and care for people.

That is so NOT fair!

Sometimes, girls are taught in nunneries. Girls who become nuns have the option to continue their studies for the rest of their lives and some go on to make great contributions to knowledge.

Being at school forever? No thanks!

OUT IN THE FIELDS
WORKING THE LAND

Most children don't go to school at all. Instead, they work outside all day, looking after the crops. Now the crops are ripe, everyone is busy harvesting them.

"It looks like such hard work!" says Jake.

"You think putting your socks on is hard work," says Lula.

The land beyond the castle walls is split into three large fields. Each field is divided into thin strips.

One field is left "fallow," with no crops growing in it, to allow the land to rest.

People can rent strips of land in each field from the baron in order to grow their own food.

> They also have to work on the baron's land.

> People pay to grow their own food?

There are woods too, for people to gather firewood to heat their homes.

> Watch out for wild boars and wolves!

> I don't want to end up like Little Red Riding Hood's grandma!

> Er... we might give the woods a miss actually.

OUCH!
GOING TO THE DOCTOR

Lula has hurt her finger and needs a bandage—but they don't have adhesive bandages in the Middle Ages!

"We have treatments for all sorts of diseases," says Hubert.

"Do they work?" asks Lula.

"Er... sometimes," says Eloise.

"We are lucky because we can see the baron's personal doctor, called a physician," says Hubert.

"We believe that four bodily fluids, called humors, control what sort of person you are—cheerful, grumpy, sad, or quiet. People get ill when their humors are out of balance," says the physician.

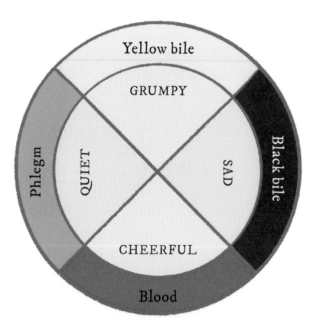

To make you well again, the physician will remove the excess humor.

If you have too much blood, he will use leeches to suck it out of you.

Who needs medicine when you can use vampire worms?! Genius!

Doctors thought they could tell which humor a patient had too much of by looking at their pee.

 **BAD NEWS!**

You're ill in the Middle Ages.

 GOOD NEWS!

The doctor doesn't think you have a problem with your humors. Instead, they blame your illness on "miasma," or BAD AIR.

 BAD NEWS!

To get rid of bad air, you need even worse air, so they make you sit on a dung heap.

 Want an operation? Go to the hairdresser!

In the Middle Ages, hairdressers did more than cut hair—they did operations, too! Today, a few barbershops still have a red and white pole outside. The red represents blood and the white represents bandages!

You'll need a doctor when we catch you!

I just need a bandage!

I'm having a BAD AIR day!

Bacon fat and flour heals bruises!

Wearing a magpie's beak around your neck cures a toothache!

Mustard and onion up your nose will stop it from running!

HELP!

Oh wait, we brought bandages with us!

NOW YOU TELL ME!

PICK A JOB!
FIGHT OR WORK?

Being a squire was a lot less fun than Jake and Lula had hoped, and they didn't enjoy working in the fields either. They know all about craftspeople, nuns, and doctors now, so what other jobs are there in the Middle Ages?

"Maybe I could run a leech farm?" says Jake.

"You can't just choose any job you like. There are many rules that we all follow," says Eloise. "Most people must do the same job as their parents."

"That's not fair!" says Jake.

"This is the Middle Ages, remember—nothing is fair," says Lula.

"Jobs are divided into three groups…" says Hubert.

Those Who Fight

The King or Queen

Make all the important decisions about running the country.

Lead their soldiers in battle.

Own all the land and directly control their own royal estates (areas of land), which pay for the royal household and daily business of running the country.

The Peers—Dukes, Counts, and Barons

Give the king or queen advice.

Help run parts of the country.

Provide soldiers and horses in time of war.

Knights, Esquires, and Gentlemen

Trained soldiers or lords of manors with smaller estates. They pay taxes to the royal family.

Being queen? A powerful job for a woman!

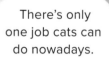

There's only one job cats can do nowadays.

What's that?

Those Who Work

Merchants
Trade in goods from different parts of the country and abroad.

Physicians and Lawyers

Shopkeepers, Tailors, Bakers, Butchers, Surgeons, and Craftspeople

Farmworkers
Farmworkers are either "free" (they rent their own land from the baron and pay tithes) or "unfree" (they have to work the baron's land).

"I did that. It's EXHAUSTING," says Jake.

"Try doing it your whole life," says Hubert. "THAT'S exhausting."

Traveling Minstrels, Salespeople, Fortune-tellers, and Knife-sharpeners

Writers and Makers of Books

And here are some more jobs for women!

Jeanne de Montbaston made beautiful books in her workshop in Paris.

Christine de Pizan was the court writer for King Charles VI of France.

Servants
Servants might get bossed around, but the servants of important people can boss other people around too!

Beggars
Not everyone was able to get a job. Some had to depend on asking people for money and food.

Mouse-catching!

WORKING FOR GOD
THOSE WHO PRAY

Jake and Lula have noticed how many religious buildings there are in the Middle Ages and they want to know more.

People follow many different religions all over the world, including Islam and Judaism. In this part of Europe, most people are Christians and worship in churches. They ask the baron's chaplain—his personal priest—to explain more.

The Pope
Head of the Church.

Cardinals
Elect the pope and help him run the Church.

Archbishops
Oversee large areas called dioceses.

Bishops
Oversee one diocese, which contains many parishes.

Priest
Oversees one parish.

Cathedrals

A cathedral is a very grand church.

It is a bishop's headquarters.

It took 50 years to build and cost a fortune.

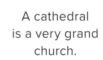

Abbeys, Monasteries, and Nunneries

Some men become monks and some women become nuns. They live in religious communities. They study, worship, and help to take care of those in need.

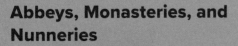

I'm a friar and I don't even cook.

Many abbeys and cathedrals contain relics—things that were important to a holy person. People who come from far away to see these relics are called pilgrims and their journey is called a pilgrimage.

Relics? After a long journey all I want to see is a comfy chair and some cookies!

He's here somewhere, I can feel it!

We just need to keep looking...

Parish Church

Every village has its own church where people gather regularly for worship. It is where churchgoers are baptized, married, and buried.

The walls and windows of a church are decorated with statues and pictures—telling stories from the Bible for people who can't read.

The German nun, Hildegard of Bingen, wrote poetry and music, and made discoveries in science and medicine.

 GOOD NEWS!

You've decided to become a monk. You can study and serve the community.

 BAD NEWS!

That means you've promised to live a simple life with no luxuries.

 GOOD NEWS!

Although you don't have money, your monastery does. Over time, people have given it so much money and land that you'll still live very well!

TOP OF THE HEROES
LEGENDARY KNIGHTS

Sir Eustace, the baron's bravest knight, comes riding by on his horse.

"He looks so cool," says Jake.
"Maybe I'd still like to be a knight after all."

Eloise introduces Lula and Jake to Sir Eustace.

"Why did you become a knight?" Lula asks.

"Because of all the wonderful stories of knights I was told when I was your age," he answers. "Here are my favorites. See which you like best."

KING ARTHUR

In his castle, Camelot, there was a Round Table for his knights to sit at. The table was round to show that all the knights were equal.

SIR LANCELOT

Bravest of the Knights of the Round Table, and King Arthur's best friend, until love drove him to break his oath of loyalty to King Arthur.

SIR GALAHAD

The purest of the knights, he succeeded in the greatest quest and found the Holy Grail.

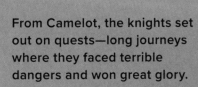

From Camelot, the knights set out on quests—long journeys where they faced terrible dangers and won great glory.

They'd get there way quicker on a train or airplane.

What are these "trains" and "airplanes" you speak of?

ST. GEORGE

HELP!

Rescued a princess from a fearsome dragon.

SIEGFRIED

Bathed in dragon's blood, which protected him from attack, but a leaf fell on his back and that patch became his weak spot.

I am a dragon! ROARRR!!

Well, we're not knights! Run!

Look! Girls are just as brave as boys.

There are stories of brave warriors, just like knights, from all over the world.

MUIRISC

Legendary ruler in Ireland. Renowned for her courage, she was a famous warrior, sea captain, and leader of men.

HUA MULAN

When war came to China, her father was too old to fight, so she took his place. Hua Mulan fought bravely for 10 years. The emperor wanted to reward her but she just wanted to go home.

THE AMAZONS

Fearsome female warriors in Greek mythology. Skilled in archery, horseback riding, and war, they lived at the edge of the known world.

KNIGHTS AROUND THE WORLD
HEROES EVERYWHERE

As Lula and Jake have seen, tales of brave warriors are told all over the world.

"Wow!" says Lula. "But are they just stories or are there real knights, doing really brave things, in other parts of the world too?"

"Of course there are!" says Sir Eustace. "Look!"

Flowering Knights or Hwarang

Noble warriors from ancient Korea, trained in the arts as well as fighting.

Bound by honor, duty, and brotherhood.

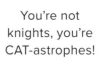

I am Clawdia the Great, most fearsome and skillful knight of the Cat-Kingdom!

I am Sir Tibert of the Noble Order of the Golden Whiskers.

You're not knights, you're CAT-astrophes!

Usama ibn Munqidh

A great *faris* (Muslim knight) and poet.

Grew up in the castle of Shayzar in Syria.

Wrote the story of his life, serving many lords in many battles.

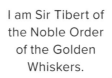

Mubarizun

The most fearsome warriors in the early Islamic world.

Before any battle, they would fight the champions of the enemy army in single combat.

The Eso Ikoyi

Military elite of the Yoruba empire of Oyo in West Africa.

Famous for their code of honor, called Emi Omo Eso.

Kheshig

The most skillful soldiers in the Mongol empire (one of the largest empires in history, stretching from the Sea of Japan to Eastern Europe).

Rewarded with money and honors.

Personal bodyguards of Genghis Khan, founder of the empire.

> Male soldiers don't have to look attractive, why should female soldiers?

Wonhwa ("Original Flowers")

Three hundred girls from the ancient kingdom of Silla, in Korea.

Chosen for their beauty and battle skills.

Samurai

A powerful class of warriors from Japan.

Served a lord and lived in his castle.

Fearsome in battle and bound by a code of honor, called Bushido.

Samurai armor is made of iron plates so it can move easily.

> Is their armor less heavy than yours?

> Much less. Their swords are sharper too!

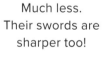

Ronin (Wandering Samurai)

When the samurais' lord died and had no heir to take his place, the samurai became "ronin" (knights without a lord) and were left to travel all over Japan, fighting for many different masters and armies.

MAKING HISTORY
THE GREAT KNIGHTS OF THE PAST

"So knights exist all over the world!" says Lula.

"History is full of brave people," says Sir Eustace.

"Who are the most famous knights of all?" asks Jake.

"There's a long list," replies Sir Eustace, "but here are a few whose names will be remembered forever."

RODRIGO DÍAZ DE VIVAR,
"EL CID"

Spanish knight who fought for both Christian and Muslim armies. Ruled over a city in which people from different cultures could live together in peace.

WILLIAM MARSHAL,
ENGLAND'S BEST KNIGHT

A successful tournament knight who went on to fight for five different English kings.

BERTRAND DU GUESCLIN,
"THE EAGLE
OF BRITTANY"

French national hero. Fought bravely against the English in the Hundred Years' War.

JOAN OF ARC

A farmer's daughter who became patron saint of France. She wasn't a knight, but her courage and faith inspired armies. Other women were just as brave as knights such as...

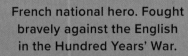

That's a LOT of kings!

MATILDA OF CANOSSA

Ruler of Tuscany, in Northern Italy. Fought for the pope and to defend her lands against the Emperor Henry IV. Known as "the Great Countess" for her strength and bravery.

ISABELLA OF CASTILE

First queen of a united Spain. Appeared in full armor to encourage her troops in battle. Encouraged explorers to go on voyages of discovery.

She looks very grand, but that armor was still cleaned with pee!

Chivalry

"Knights are not just warriors," Sir Eustace explains. "We are all bound by a code of honor, called chivalry. To be a knight is to be brave and fair, loyal and generous, to protect the weak and fight for what's good. Sometimes, knights join together in orders of chivalry such as these."

Order of the Garter

Founded by Edward III of England.

To help Edward become king of France.

Celebrated with feasting and jousting.

Order of the Golden Fleece

Founded by Philip, Duke of Burgundy.

To honor the noble order of knighthood.

Knights would be asked about going to war, and disputes between knights would be settled by the order, not law courts.

Order of the Star

Founded by King John II of France.

To reward loyalty to the king and protect France from the English.

Knights swore never to retreat from a battle.

Gotcha!

But there's two of you—that's against the rules of chivalry!

45

LET THE GAMES BEGIN!

CELEBRATING WITH A TOURNAMENT

The kids hear the sound of trumpets from outside.

"The baron is celebrating his return home with a tournament," says Sir Eustace. "I have to go and get ready."

"We don't want to miss this!" says Jake.

They follow the crowds who are gathering to watch.

Where has that pesky mouse gone?

Something's wriggling inside my armor and tickling me!

Shhh!

Jousting started as battle practice—many battles were won by a lot of knights charging at once.

The little wooden fence in the middle is called the "tilt."

Knights charge on the right-hand side of the tilt.

In England, King Edward I banned the spectators from having weapons in case they wanted to join in too!

A knight is allowed three lances. If they break all three and there's still no winner, the fight continues on foot with blunt swords.

GOOD NEWS!

You're a knight in a joust—everyone's turned out to see how brave you are.

BAD NEWS!

You're facing a fearsome rival.

GOOD NEWS!

The pointy end of your rival's lance is capped.

BAD NEWS!

Being hit with a lance still delivers an almighty THWACK!

The people who are in charge—such as the baron and his wife—watch the joust from a covered stand.

That poor knight lost his joust! What happens to him now?

He could lose his armor and his horse. He might even be taken prisoner and ransomed!

Squires are on hand to supply their knight with new weapons and armor.

He wants to join in! Don't tell Edward I.

Lady's Favor

Some knights fight to prove their love. They wear a "favor" (a ribbon, a handkerchief, or a glove) to show which lady they are fighting for. If they win, they might get a kiss.

Ugh! I'd make sure I lost.

GOOD NEWS!

If you win, you might get money or jewels.

BAD NEWS!

The prize in one tournament wasn't money or jewels—it was a peacock!

A GOODBYE FEAST

It's getting late and Jake and Lula's tummies are rumbling again. The baron is holding a great feast in the hall and Lula and Jake are invited to join as guests.

"I can't wait for the big feast!" says Jake. "Will there be pizza?"

"What's pizza?" asks Hubert.

"Huh?! No pizza? What are we going to eat?" asks Jake.

"The baron's favorite food is pork, eggs, currants, and dates boiled together in a bladder, which is then sliced and eaten in sauce."

"Ugh!" says Jake.

"Will there be other food to eat besides... er... bladder?" asks Lula.

"There will be lots of boiled, baked, and roasted meat," says Hubert, "as well as fish, baked and stewed fruit, and cheese."

Meat is cooked with dried fruit, and plenty of spices such as cinnamon, cumin, licorice, ginger, coriander, nutmeg, and cloves.

Forks are used in the kitchen but most people won't use forks to eat with for another 100 years.

Food arrives in sharing bowls. People serve themselves. It's bad manners to take all the best bits for yourself.

At last! I'm starving after running around all day!

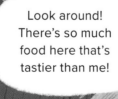

Look around! There's so much food here that's tastier than me!

He might be right. What's that delicious smell?

People are seated in order of their importance. The baron and his wife have the best spot—sitting right in the middle of the most important table. They will be served first and have the best view of the entertainment.

Minstrels play music from a special gallery.

Henry II of England had a jester called Ronald the Farter. Every Christmas he had to perform "one jump and whistle and one fart."

Finally, a job I have the right experience for. I want to be a jester!

Table manners?! It's just like back home.

TABLE MANNERS

Wash your hands before and after dinner.

Take food OFF your knife to eat it.

Don't fill your mouth with food.

Don't wipe your mouth on your sleeve—use a napkin.

No spitting or belching at the table!

Maybe we could be friends instead?

You're right. Roast chicken tastes so much better than mouse!

I'd love to! My name is Maurice—pleased to meet you.

BEDTIME!

Jake and Lula have had so many adventures in the Middle Ages, but now it's time for their sleepover.

"These beds have curtains!" says Jake. "We can play hide-and-seek!"

"The curtains are designed to keep you warm in a drafty castle," explains Hubert.

"And besides," says Eloise. "You've just given away your hiding place!"

"What shall we do then?" asks Lula. "I'm far too excited to sleep."

Some candy from the feast for our own jester, Jake?

"Would you like to take a souvenir home?" asks Eloise.

"I'd like that balloon thing the jester has please," says Jake.

"His bladder, you mean?" says Hubert.

"As long as you promise not to bop me on the head with it," says Lula.

"Oh all right!" says Jake.

"I'd like a knight's shield please," says Lula. "If I hold it up in front of my face, I won't have to watch Jake's 'jump, whistle, and fart' jester dance."

Do you think the jester would mind if I stole some of his jokes?

You're a natural jester, Jake—you're always making me laugh!

What would you like to take back?

Nothing. I just wish we'd made friends with Maurice sooner. Think of all the fun we could have had together!

51

THE SLEEPOVER'S OVER!

THANKS FOR HAVING US

The next morning, it's time for our travelers to go home.

"That was a very comfy bed," says Lula, "until the bedbugs got me."

"Hubert and Eloise, you must come and visit us sometime," says Jake.

"Oh yes," says Lula. "I'd love to show you phones, and the games you can play on them, and trains. They're like carriages without horses that whiz along rails at 100 miles an hour."

"No one can travel that fast!" says Hubert.

"Just you wait," says Lula.

"But how will we visit you?" asks Eloise.

"Time travel," say Lula and Jake. "It's easy...

You do a little wiggle...

This looks like an interesting dance.

...and you touch the ground.

Then wrinkle your nose while you spin around.

You shake your hips, then you jump off the ground. And just like that...

You're home!"

Oops!

52